MILFORD & ME

_In O._

Patrick 2015

MILFORD & ME

PATRICK LANE

ILLUSTRATED BY BONNIE McLEAN

COTEAU BOOKS

Designed by Joyce Sotski
Printed and bound in Canada by Hignell Printing Ltd.

We gratefully acknowledge the assistance of the Saskatchewan Arts Board
and the Canada Council in the publication of this book.

**Saskatchewan
Arts Board**

Canadian Cataloguing in Publication Data

Lane, Patrick, 1939–
   Milford and me

   Poem.
   ISBN: 0-919926-96-7 (bound); 0-919926-97-5 (pbk.)

I. McLean, Bonnie, 1958–. II. Title.
PS8523.A64M5 1989   jC811'.54   C89-098078-0
PZ8.3.L364M5 1989

coteau books

209–1945 Scarth Street
Regina, Saskatchewan
S4P 2H2

For Eric and Jeremy and my godson Ben

My favourite small turtle is Milford.
He likes grasshoppers, roses, and beans.
He lives in my garden all summer
and he always says just what he means.

When you talk to a turtle, says Milford,
leave spaces between what you say.
Go patiently, slowly, and easy,
because fast only gets in the way.

But especially when talking to turtles,
remember, speak only in rhyme.
Words are important to turtles.
They've been here a very long time.

Milford has wonderful stories.
He should cause he's lived very long.
All from the time before people
when turtles were terribly strong.

I held up the world once, says Milford.
You wouldn't believe it to see
a turtle as small now as I am
but it's true, it's as true as can be.

The world once sat on my green shell.
All the stars and the earth and the sea.
Now that was a job for a turtle,
says Milford, and I must agree.

Who holds it up now? I ask Milford.
Who knows? says small Milford to me.
It could be a flower or grass blade
or a grumbily fat bumblebee.

Then he went to sleep under a lettuce
and I looked very hard at his shell.
Imagine the world sitting on it!
And what if it suddenly fell?

And right then a bumblebee stumbled
as bumblebees do in the air.
I hope there's a turtle like Milford
and I hope he will always be there,

holding the stars on his green shell,
all the stars and the rocks and the sea,
a brother or sister of Milford,
not a stumbily fat bumblebee.

Imagine a bumblebee fumbling
and the world falling off of her wings?
I sure hope there's a turtle like Milford
to look after all of those things.

Why are names? I ask Milford the Turtle.
I mean, why is a beetle called that?
Why is a bird called a humming?
And why is my cat called a cat?

A name, says small Milford, is being.
A thing to say you are the one.
Names are like numbers with feeling,
the shape of a tree in the sun.

Before there were names there was nothing.
Nobody knew how to play.
There were fighting and fooling and bad times
till a turtle decided to say:

From now on my name will be turtle
and the world stopped a moment or three.
Then a bird said, This is what I am,
then a rock, then a fish, then a bee.

Then everything named itself I AM.
Each thing was different from each.
The mountains were names in a tall way,
and the edge of a lake was a beach.

And that is why everything's different
from a rose to a cow to a leek.
Before we were names we were nothing.
Just look at the days of the week.

Monday is mostly a moon-time
and Tuesday's a lady in white.
Wednesday is hanging-from-trees day
and Thursday is warriors who fight.

Friday will love you forever
and Saturday's home without harm.
Sunday is gardens and sleeping.
The days are all made out of charms.

We're more than just numbers and adding.
Each one of us while we are here
is a name that's magically our name
and so we have nothing to fear.

I call myself Milford the Turtle,
someone who's always your friend.
That's a good enough reason for naming
and it always will be, till the end.

Names are far better than nothing
cause nothing is nowhere at all.
A name is a me and a you thing
and that's why I come when you call.

Milford, are there monsters in water,
down in the weeds and the rocks?
I'd like to meet up with a monster
and hear what it says when it talks.

There are monsters, says Milford quite slowly.
I knew some when I was first small.
Some live down under water.
Some are short, some are fat, some are tall.

I have a good friend who's a monster.
She is kindly and really quite old.
She lives in a big yellow tulip.
She's always been friendly I'm told.

The spiders weave all of her blankets
and she sits in a red carrot chair.
I like her a lot, says small Milford.
As far as I know she's still there.

We walk a long way to the tulips,
way down at the end of the yard.
At last we get down to the flowers.
By then we are both very tired.

I knock on the tulip quite gently.
A tulip-house is very small!
A voice says, I'm glad you could visit.
I'm glad you could come for a call.

Then out of the tulip comes Mavis.
She's blue from her nose to her knees.
On her feet she wears bright orange slippers.
Her hair is as green as the trees.

She changes shape every few minutes.
Her voice is a high and a low.
She laughs like the colour of roses,
and her eyes are two tiny rainbows.

I sit with small Milford and Mavis
not wanting to wander about.
At first she is hidden and quiet,
but after a while she comes out.

We talk about climbing up mountains
and living down under the sea
and why everyone hated monsters
when monsters are nice as can be.

Most monsters are really quite tiny,
says Mavis to Milford and me.
My sister's the size of an apple
and my brother's as small as a pea.

You shouldn't be frightened by monsters.
They're really nice people to meet.
Then she offers us butterfly pancakes
with bumblebee butter and beets.

I know now that monsters aren't scary.
I know they're as nice as can be.
Like dragonflies, turtles, and sparrows.
They're friendly like you and like me.

We walk along down by the turnips.
There is no one but Milford and me.
We've been sharing a cucumber sandwich
in the shade of a very tall pea.

There are things I don't know about, Milford,
I say when I take my last bite.
Who is God and where is He living?
Is God in the day or the night?

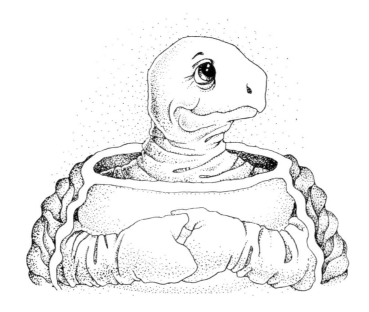

It can be quite confusing, says Milford,
to explain God and all sorts of things,
like maple trees, wagons, and turtles,
and baseball, and robins, and swings.

You see, God is more than just seeing,
or having, or being, or not.
God isn't a *He* or *She* thing.
God's an *Everything*, so I was taught

when I was a very large turtle
back in the days before days.
God's an inside, an outside, an all-thing,
a backwards, a forwards, a maze.

But mostly God is a *Not-Name*.
A word that is never a word.
Something you can't put your eyes on,
like a song when you can't see the bird.

I thought about Milford and *Not-Names*,
I thought and I thought while I sat,
and I know now I know what I'm knowing,
so I think I'll go play with my cat

cause if God is an *Everywhere-Always*
then my cat is a part of God too,
like Milford and my mother and father
and all of my best friends and you.

Small Milford likes talking to Nowlan.
I know it sounds strange he does that.
He talks very quickly, says Milford.
He's a good friend. He's Nowlan the Cat.

You can speak with a person, says Milford,
about marigolds, monsters, and birds,
but Nowlan knows all about night-time,
about darkness and various verbs

that are all about hunting and hiding,
and stalking and leaping and jumps.
A cat is all verbs, says small Milford.
He's a moving without any bumps.

A verb is a going or coming,
a moving from darkness to light.
A climbing, a falling, a flying,
a somewhere to nowhere delight

that is scary if you don't know him
or if you're surprised by his paw
when he suddenly lies down beside you
and tells you about what he saw

when he climbed to the top of the chimney
and looked around all of the night
while you and I still were sleeping
wrapped up in our blankets all tight.

The Author, Patrick Lane

Well-known Canadian poet, Patrick Lane, has published extensively during a career that spans more than thirty years. *Milford & Me* is his first book for children. His twelve adult poetry collections include *Selected Poems* (Oxford, 1978), *The Measure* (Black Moss, 1980), *Old Mother* (Oxford, 1981), *A Linen Crow, A Caftan Magpie* (Thistledown, 1983), and *Poems, New and Selected* (Oxford, 1987).

His poetry has appeared in most major journals in Canada and the U.S., with additional publication in Europe, Asia and South America. His work has been published in most major Canadian anthologies, including *A Sudden Radiance* (Coteau, 1987).

During his writing career, Patrick has won several prestigious literary awards. In 1979, he won the Governor General's Award for poetry, for *Selected Poems*. His *Poems, New and Selected* won the Canadian Authors Association award for poetry in 1988. In 1989, Patrick was recognized with a Gold for poetry by the National Magazine Awards. He has also been the recipient of several senior Canada Council writing grants.

A native of British Columbia, Patrick has spent most of the 1980s in Saskatchewan either writing or teaching. He is the father of five children and grandfather of two young boys, Eric and Jeremy, to whom, along with his godson Ben, *Milford & Me* is dedicated.

Patrick is currently working on a collection of short fiction and a book of poetry. A new collection of poetry, *Winter*, will be published by Coteau Books in 1990.

The Illustrator, Bonnie McLean

Milford & Me is also a first for Bonnie McLean—the first book she has illustrated for children. Bonnie holds a degree in art history from the University of Alberta and a diploma in dance from Grant MacEwan College. She teaches dance and currently lives in British Columbia, following a year's sojourn in Scotland.